More books about Kipper:

First published in 2014 by Hodder Children's Books
This paperback edition first published in 2015

Copyright © Mick Inkpen 2014

Hodder Children's Books
338 Euston Road, London NW1 3BH

Hodder Children's Books Australia
Level 17/207 Kent Street, Sydney, NSW 2000

A catalogue record of this book is
available from the British Library.

ISBN: 978 1 444 91819 9
10 9 8 7 6 5 4 3 2 1

Printed in China

Hodder Children's Books is a
division of Hachette Children's Books.
An Hachette UK company.
www.hachette.co.uk

Kipper's
Little Friends

Mick Inkpen

A division of Hachette Children's Books

Arnold was proudly showing
Kipper his new toy baby owl.
It was very small.
And grey. And fluffy.
'We could call your owl. . .
Small Grey Fluffy Owl,'
said Kipper.
It was not a very
inventive name.
A bit long too.
But Arnold
seemed pleased.

'Big Owl . . . and Small Grey Fluffy Owl,' said Kipper.

'I wonder what a baby owl is called?' said Kipper.
'You are a baby pig.
And a baby pig is called a piglet.
So perhaps a baby owl is called. . .
an Owlet!'

Kipper looked at his computer.

'Yes!' said Kipper.
'A baby owl is an owlet.'

'And look! A baby frog is. . .
a froglet!'

He read some more.

'And a baby hedgehog is. . .
a hoglet!'

K ipper was very pleased with himself.

'Piglet. Owlet. Froglet. Hoglet,' he said.
'Let's go to the park and see if we can find some hoglets and froglets!'

They couldn't find any hoglets in the park. And there were no froglets in the pond.

Just some wriggly things in the stinky mud.

But the ducks were there as usual. And five baby ducks were paddling in the pond too.

Arnold wondered if
Small Grey Fluffy Owl
would like to paddle with them...

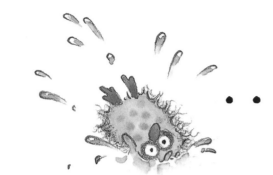

...splish!

Small Grey Fluffy Owl spun slowly on his back, and began to sink.

The baby ducks, thinking he was a piece of bread, paddled over to dabble at him.

'Shoooo!' said Kipper, and dipped his net into the water.

Small Grey Fluffy Owl
wasn't very fluffy any more.
And he seemed even smaller
than before.
 A bit stinky too.

 But Arnold didn't seem
to notice. He had discovered
something interesting in the net.

 tiny froglet!

It crawled onto
Arnold's finger...

stared at him for a while...

then hopped onto his nose...

and jumped back into the pond...

...ploop!

They sat on the swings, swooshing backwards and forwards, while Kipper spun Small Grey Fluffy Owl around to dry him out.

'What is the name for a baby duck?' said Kipper. 'Piglet. Owlet. Froglet. Hoglet. It must be. . .

ducklet!'

It didn't sound right.

Back home Kipper looked
at his computer again.
'Silly me! A baby duck is
called a **duckling!**
Of course it is!' said Kipper.

'And look, Arnold!
A baby goose is called a **gosling.**
I didn't know that.

And goslings are grey and fluffy too!'

They drew pictures of all the baby animals and wrote the names underneath.

owlet

froglet

piglet

hoglet

duckling   gosling

Then Kipper drew a picture of himself and wrote **dog**.

dog

'What was I when I was little?' said Kipper.
'Was I a. . .

doglet. . .
or a dogling?'

Silly Kipper. He had forgotten the name for a baby dog.

Do you know the name for a baby dog?

Of course you do.
A baby dog is a. . .

...puppy.

And this is what
Kipper looked like
when Big Owl was
brand new,
and Kipper was
just a puppy.

'My children absolutely LOVE all of Mick Inkpen's books, and I still love reading Kipper to them, even when it's for the hundredth time. . .'

CRESSIDA COWELL

'He is the perfect pup to grow up with. . .'

HILARY McKAY

'Storytelling at its best.' DAVID MELLING